SARA O'LEARY

with illustrations by
JULIE MORSTAD

Published in 2012 by Simply Read Books www.simplyreadbooks.com
Text © 2011 Sara O'Leary · Illustrations © 2011 Julie Morstad

Library and Archives Canada Cataloguing in Publication
O'Leary, Sara
          When I was small / written by Sara O'Leary ;
illustrated by Julie Morstad.
ISBN 978-1-897476-38-3
          I. Morstad, Julie II. Title.
PS8579.L293W45 2011   jC813'.54   C2010-905682-5

We gratefully acknowledge for their financial support of our publishing program the Canada Council for the Arts, the BC Arts Council, and the Government of Canada through the Canada Book Fund (CBF).

Manufactured in China
This product conforms to CPSIA 2008

Book design by Robin Mitchell-Cranfield for hundreds & thousands

10 9 8 7 6 5 4 3 2

Simply Read Books

WHEN I WAS SMALL

SARA O'LEARY

with illustrations by

JULIE MORSTAD

Henry wishes he had known his parents
when they were small.
Tell me a story, he begs his mother.
Tell me about when you were small, too.

When I was small, says his mother, my name was Dorothea. But because the name was too big for me, everyone called me Dot.

When I was small, says his mother, my doll and I wore the same size shoes.

When I was small, says his mother,
I went swimming in the birdbath.

When I was small, says his mother,
I played jump rope with a piece of yarn.

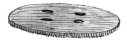

When I was small, says his mother,
I could feast on a single raspberry.

When I was small, says his mother,
I slept in a mitten.

When I was small, says his mother,
the cat once mistook me for one of her kittens.

When I was small, says his mother,
I could wear a daisy for a sun hat.

When I was small, says his mother,
my best friend was a ladybug.

When I was small, says his mother, my father built me a doll's house.

One bed was too hard....

One bed was too soft....

But one bed was just right.

When I was small, says his mother,
I couldn't wait to grow up.
Because I knew one day I would have
a small boy of my own.

And you could tell him stories, says Henry.

Yes, says his mother.

And I would tell him stories, because in stories
we can be small together.

THE END